Published in the United States of America and its dependencies by
Oak Tree Publications, Inc.
9601 Aero Dr., Suite 202
San Diego, CA 92123

This edition copyright © Templar Publishing Ltd 1985
Text copyright © Richard Carlisle 1985

ISBN 0-86679-045-4

Library of Congress Cataloging-in-Publication Data

Carlisle, Richard, 1949–
Who's afraid of ghosts?

(Who's afraid)
Summary: A child ponders all the places that may be
concealing the ghosts he fears, until his parents
convince him that ghosts are not real.
[1. Ghosts—Fiction.   2. Fear—Fiction]   I. Anstey,
David, ill.   II. Title.   III. Title: Who is afraid of
ghosts?   IV. Series: Carlisle, Richard, 1949–
Who's afraid.
PZ7.C216375Whg   1987   [E]   86-21797
ISBN 0-86679-045-4

This book was devised and produced by Templar Publishing Ltd,
107 High Street, Dorking, Surrey

Color separations by Positive Colour Ltd, Maldon, Essex

Printed and bound by New Interlitho, Milan, Italy.

Dedicated to Maxine and Sam who were never really afraid

WHO'S AFRAID
—— of ghosts? ——

Written by Richard Carlisle
Illustrated by David Anstey

Brett Daniel
from
Nana + Pop Pop French
Christmas 1991

Oak Tree Publications, Inc.
San Diego, California

I'm afraid of ghosts
and ghostly things that hide
in corners of the cupboard
and in the dark outside.

Ghosts look quite fantastic,
a little like a blurr,
although I've never seen one
to be absolutely sure.

Ghosts might look like shadows
or sometimes like a sheet,
white and waving in the wind
– I hope we never meet.

But if we do, I have a plan,
I'll bravely shut my eyes
then hide beneath the bedclothes
to help with my disguise.

Ghosts are sometimes smoky,
floating near the floor,
or sometimes on the ceiling
and sometimes by the door.

But really ghosts are wispy
which means they're made of air.
They run through walls imagining
the walls aren't really there.

Ghosts are also silent.
That means they make no sound,
instead you sort of feel them
which makes you turn around.

But when you look much harder
you find the ghost has fled.
That's probably because the ghost
has gone back to his bed.

Imagine what a ghostly life
would seem like in the cold.
You couldn't wrap up warm at all
and do as you were told.

Without a fire to sit by
you couldn't toast your toes,
without a proper handkerchief
you couldn't blow your nose.

It might seem rather foolish,
with lights in every room,
to think a ghost is waiting
upstairs behind the gloom.

But people say be careful
in case you get a shock –
ghosts are awfully tricky
at sliding through the lock.

One night when I was little
I crept upstairs to bed
when suddenly a funny thought
came swimming in my head.

What if a ghost was waiting?
What if I did not see?
So quickly closing both my eyes,
I tripped and hurt my knee.

My Dad just says I'm silly,
but what if I'm surprised
by ghostly teeth that tell me
a ghost has just arrived?

Quite recently it happened.
He came to say goodnight,
but just before he reached my room
I saw a ghostly light.

I quickly raced across the floor
as fast as I did dare,
then hid myself beneath the bed
and came up just for air.

He thought that I was playing games
or looking for a ball.
He didn't know a ghost was near,
just behind my wall.

I pointed to the window
and told my Mom beware,
but when my Dad looked all around
the ghost just wasn't there.

So tucked in bed they told me
that ghosts aren't real at all
– I know this is a fact because
my Dad's extremely tall.

From high above me he can see
all kinds of things I can't,
and he has never seen a ghost
and neither has my Aunt.

It makes me smile now that I know.
In fact, I sometimes laugh.
If ghosts were real they'd stay at home
and send a photograph.

The End